Sea Horses

BY KARA L. LAUGHLIN

childsworld.com

Published by The Child's World®
1980 Lookout Drive • Mankato, MN 56003-1705
800-599-READ • www.childsworld.com

DESIGN ELEMENTS
© creatOR76/Shutterstock.com: porthole
© keren-seg/Shutterstock.com: water

PHOTO CREDITS
© Andrea Izzotti/Shutterstock.com: 16-17; Doug Perrine/NPL/
Minden Pictures: 18-19; Frolova_Elena/Shutterstock.com: 6-7;
Kjeld Friis/Shutterstock.com: 11, 20-21; Kristina Vackova/
Shutterstock.com: 12-13; Rich Carey/Shutterstock.com: 5, 14;
Suwat Sirivutcharungchit/Shutterstock.com: cover, 1; Syafiq
Adnan/Shutterstock.com: 8-9

ISBN: 9781503816886
LCCN: 2016945603

Printed in the United States of America
PA02326

NOTE FOR PARENTS AND TEACHERS

The Child's World® helps early readers develop their
informational-reading skills by providing easy-to-read books
that fascinate them and hold their interest. Encourage new
readers by following these simple ideas:

BEFORE READING

- Page briefly through the book. Discuss the photos. What
  does the reader think he or she will learn in this book? Let
  the child ask questions.
- Look at the glossary together. Discuss the words.

READ THE BOOK

- Now read the book together, or let the child read the book
  independently.

AFTER READING

- Urge the child to think more. Ask questions such as, "What
  things are different among the animals shown in this book?"

Contents

Strange Fish

Do you see that strange fish hiding in the sea grass? It is a sea horse. Sea horses are fish. They have **fins**. They use **gills** to breathe.

Did you know?

Sea horses do not have scales like other fish.

Life in the Grass

Sea horses live all over the world. They live near coasts. They hide in sea grasses and **coral** that grow there.

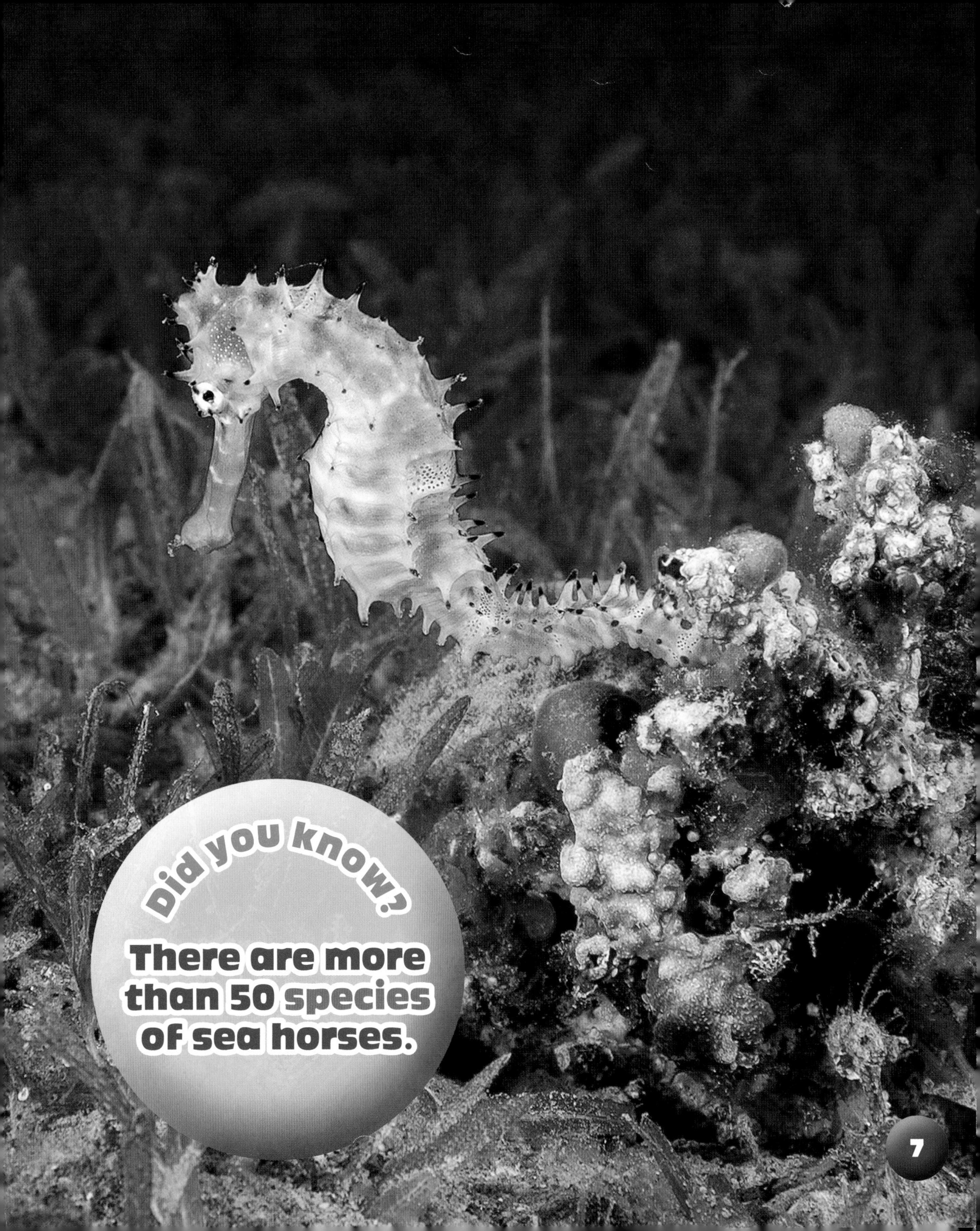

Did you know?

There are more than 50 species of sea horses.

Did you know?

Sea horses can be up to 14 inches (36 centimeters) long.

Blending In

Sea horses are good at hiding. They are **camouflaged** to blend in with their homes.

Slow Swimmers

Sea horses are poor swimmers. They are slow. They stay near their hiding places.

Hanging On

Sea horses have strong tails. They can grab coral or sea grass. When the sea gets rough, sea horses hold on tight.

Did you know?

Sea horses do not chew. They suck in their food like a vacuum.

Food

A sea horse eats through its long **snout**. Sea horses eat small shrimp. They eat tiny baby fish, too. Sea horses eat all day long.

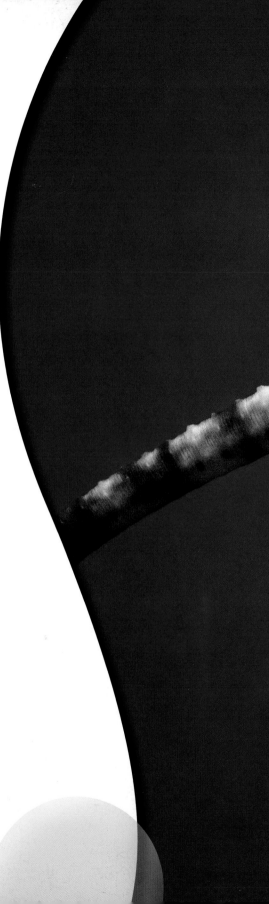

A Sea Horse Family

In a sea horse family, the father carries the eggs. He has a pouch on his belly. The eggs grow there until they are born.

Did you know?

A male can carry
up to 1,500 eggs
at one time.

Did you know?

Of 1,000 sea horse fry, only 5 will live to be adults.

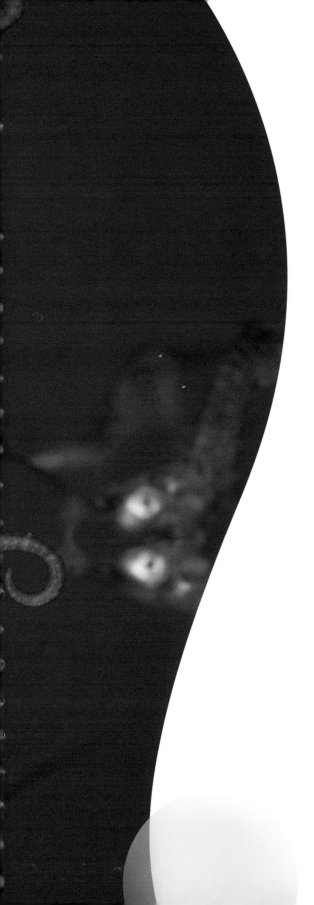

Baby sea horses are called **fry**. Many fry are born, but not many grow up. Many sea horse fry get eaten by other fish.

Sea horses are important. They add to the wonder of the sea.

Did you know?

Sea horses live for about 5 years.

GLOSSARY

camouflage (KAM-uh-flazh): Camouflage is coloring that makes something blend in with its surroundings.

coral (KOR-ull): Coral are tiny sea animals that live close together. When coral die, they leave behind rock-like clumps and mounds.

fins (FINZ): Fins are flap-like body parts that help fish move and steer as they swim through the water.

fry (FRY): Baby fish are called fry.

gills (GILZ): Gills are organs on some animals that allow the animals to breathe underwater.

snout (SNOWT): An animal's snout is where its mouth and nose are. An animal's snout sticks out from its face.

species (SPEE-sheez): A type of a certain animal. There are more than 50 species of sea horses.

TO LEARN MORE

on the Web

Visit our Web page for
lots of links about sea horses:
www.childsworld.com/links

Note to parents, teachers, and librarians:
We routinely verify our Web links to make
sure they are safe, active sites—
so encourage your readers
to check them out!

In the Library

James, Helen Foster. *Discover Sea Horses*. Ann Arbor, MI:
Cherry Lake Publishing, 2016.

Leaf, Christina. *Sea Horses*. Minneapolis, MN:
Bellwether Media, 2016.

Meister, Cari. *Sea Horses*. Minneapolis, MN:
Bullfrog Books, 2014.

INDEX

About the Author

Kara L. Laughlin is an artist and writer who lives in Virginia with her husband, three kids, two guinea pigs, and a dog. She is the author of two dozen nonfiction books for kids.